/   𝒳

JE   Schwartz, Mary Ada.
S   Spiffen, a tale of a tidy pig / Mary Ada
          Schwartz ; illustrated by Lynn Munsinger. --
          Niles, Ill. : A. Whitman, c1988.

              1 v. : ill. ; wc k-3.   88314
              SUMMARY: Spiffen, a neat pig spurned by the
          sloppy other pigs of Slobbyville, becomes a
          hero through a daring deed only a tidy pig
          could have performed.
              ISBN 0-8075-7580-1(lib. bdg.) : $11.95

                                              OCT 88

              1. Cleanliness--Fiction. 2. Pigs--Fiction.
          I. Title.
                                                     19

                                              88-15 /AC
                                                   MARC

SPIFFEN
A TALE OF A TIDY PIG

Mary Ada Schwartz

Illustrated by Lynn Munsinger

Albert Whitman & Company   Niles, Illinois

To Carolyn and Trevor, my little piglets. M.A.S.
For Sarah and Zachary. L.M.

Library of Congress Cataloging-in-Publication Data

Schwartz, Mary Ada.
    Spiffen, a tale of a tidy pig / Mary Ada Schwartz ; illustrated by
Lynn Munsinger.
        p. cm.
    Summary: Spiffen, a neat pig spurned by the sloppy other pigs of
Slobbyville, becomes a hero through a daring deed only a tidy pig
could have performed.
    ISBN 0-8075-7580-1 (lib. bdg.)
    [1. Cleanliness—Fiction. 2. Orderliness—Fiction. 3. Pigs—
Fiction.] I. Munsinger, Lynn, ill. II. Title.
PZ7.S41125Sp 1988
[E]—dc19   88-15
                                                             CIP AC

Text © 1988 by Mary Ada Schwartz
Illustrations © 1988 by Lynn Munsinger
Design by Karen Yops
Published in 1988 by Albert Whitman & Company, Niles, Illinois
Published simultaneously in Canada by General Publishing, Limited, Toronto

Once upon a time, in a far-off pigdom in the town of Slobbyville, there lived a young pig named Spiffen.

The other townspigs were grubby and dirty. They liked to eat garbage and roll in the mud. But Spiffen was different.

He was a very tidy little pig. In the morning, he brushed his teeth, washed his face, and scrubbed hard behind his ears. Then he struggled into a clean tunic, pulled his stockings up tight so they didn't wrinkle at the ankles, and buffed his boots.

After breakfast, he walked alone to school since he was
the only student who arrived on time.

At school, Spiffen used up all the erasers fixing his mistakes. "Your work is too neat. It's boring to correct," his teacher often grunted.

On the way home, the other pigs teased him:

Spiffen, Spiffen,
neat as a pin,
the Misfit of Slobbyville—
don't let him in!

Each day, Spiffen wearily wiped his feet clean as he came into the house. Mama would groan, "Here you are again, right on time for dinner! Well, I'm not ready! I've had a long day of messing up the house and soiling our clothes. I haven't had time yet to bring in the garbage."

After dinner, Spiffen went to help his father in the
workshop. He sorted the loose tools and put them neatly
away. Papa always grumbled, "Now I won't be able to find
a thing."

When Spiffen was a wee piglet, his parents had thought his tidiness was cute and funny. He would surely outgrow it, lose his manners, and chew with his mouth open as all pigs did—or so they thought.

But all Spiffen was losing was his friends. Their parents didn't like him in their homes. They were shocked by his clean clothes and shiny pink face. Behind his back, they whispered, "How can his mother let him go out like that? He's *such* a bad influence on our piglets. The other day, I caught him putting the top back *on* the peanut-butter jar and throwing *out* the garbage!" There was even talk of banishing him to the hills surrounding Slobbyville, although dragons roamed there and fed on wayward pigs.

One day, word came that His Griminess, King Hog, was searching for the sloppiest town in his pigdom. Soon he would visit Slobbyville! The excited pigs began to prepare a huge parade and feast.

Some collected bags of trash to be thrown in the streets while others sprayed slime on their windows and mud on their walls. The worst cooks heaped rotten fruit, moldy bread, and charred meat onto greasy platters that would be tossed around at the feast.

When the big day arrived, the pigs bathed in the swamp, wrinkled and stained their outfits, and smeared their faces with ketchup and chocolate pudding. For the final touch, everyone rolled in a freshly fertilized weed garden.

Everyone, that is, except Spiffen. All the preparations
upset him terribly. Mama sighed and rumpled his tunic.
"Why don't you go to your room, dear?" she said. "You can
watch the parade from there."

Soon the parade became a free-for-all. Pigs squealed and snorted as they shoved each other into puddles. Bits of litter drifted down from rooftops, and wads of crumpled paper

crunched under pig feet. Banana peels, eggshells, and apple cores were trampled into a gritty muck that squished up between pig toes. King Hog was thrilled. This was truly the sloppiest town in his pigdom!

The noise and stench drifted up to the hills surrounding
Slobbyville, where a particularly ferocious dragon slept.

And it reached Spiffen as he stood watching by his lonely window. He began to feel dizzy, and his stomach started to churn. So he did something that had soothed him in the past when the dirty habits of his fellow pigs had made him ill.

He filled a bucket with warm water. Next, he got the
sponge and bar of soap he kept hidden in his top drawer
under his neatly rolled socks. Then he went behind his
house to scrub his bicycle.

Spiffen was just starting on the handlebars when he heard
a horrible roar. It was followed by terrified screams. Peering
around his house, he saw the huge, fire-breathing dragon
blocking the path of the parade.

Spiffen heard the beast growl, "*You* should do fine for the main course." To everyone's horror, the dragon reached out and grabbed King Hog! The pigs all scrambled in different directions, squealing in fright.

King Hog was about to become a broiled pork-chop dinner! Spiffen was so shocked that he could not move.

"Now, before cooking this one, I must find some dessert," the dragon hissed. He looked around, but there was no one in sight but Spiffen.

The dragon grinned. "Here's an easy catch, and I won't even have to wash him first!" His giant teeth gleamed through the flames in his mouth, and his great grubby claws reached for Spiffen.

As the dirty, fiery beast drew closer, Spiffen did the only thing he could. He grabbed the bucket and heaved the soapy water at the dragon.

The dragon howled in pain as the bucket flipped down on his head. Then the water put out his fire! Clouds of steam from his mouth sizzled and swirled around him, frightening the monstrous beast. When he opened his mouth to roar, all that came out was a bunch of bubbles.

The dragon dropped King Hog. He turned and fled to the hills, sneezing and coughing up bubbles. Spiffen's suds had saved the day!

One by one, the other townspigs peeked out from their hiding places. They gathered around Spiffen, lifted him onto their shoulders, and carried him through the streets cheering:

> *Spiffen, Spiffen,*
> *of thee we sing.*
> *The Hero of Slobbyville*
> *has saved the king!*

The next week, there was a special ceremony. Instead of honoring Slobbyville, the sloppiest town in all the pigdom, King Hog honored Spiffen, its cleanest hero. Spiffen received a shiny gold medal in the shape of a bar of soap. His parents watched proudly. Their little misfit piglet was now famous!

By royal decree, the name of the town was changed from Slobbyville to Soapyville. From that time forth, on the king's orders, every household kept a bucket of suds ready for surprise dragon attacks.

But best of all, Spiffen was able to clean happily ever after.